Stay Away from the Swamp

Look for these SpineChillers™ Mysteries

Stay Away from the Swamp

Fred E. Katz

Thomas Nelson, Inc.
Nashville

Published in Nashville, Tennessee, by Tommy Nelson™, a division of Thomas Nelson, Inc. SpineChillers™ is a trademark of Thomas Nelson, Inc.

Scripture quoted from the *International Children's Bible, New Century Version,* copyright © 1986, 1988 by Word Publishing. Used by permission.

Library of Congress Cataloging-in-Publication Data

Katz, Fred E.
    Stay away from the swamp / Fred E. Katz—[Rev. ed.]
        p.   cm.—(SpineChillers mysteries ; 8)
    Summary: Clint and his best friend Hammer become increasingly involved in the rumors associated with the parcel of land known as the Haunted Swamp.
    ISBN 0-8499-4064-8
    [1. Swamps—Fiction. 2. Smuggling—Fiction. 3. Christian life—Fiction. 4. Horror stories.] I. Title. II. Series: Katz, Fred E. SpineChillers mysteries : 8.
PZ7.K1573Sp 1997
[Fic]—dc21   97-32229
                                         CIP
                                       AC

Printed in the United States of America

97 98 99 00 01 02 QKP 9 8 7 6 5 4 3 2 1

"Hammer? Come on in here." I set the pizza on the bar in the kitchen and opened the box. The aroma from the hot cheese, pepperoni, onions, and black olives made my mouth water. "Hey—Hammer?"

No answer.

I stood up straight. Though it was high noon on a July day, I felt a chill. It raised goose bumps on my arms.

Where was everybody? Why had the house gone silent? It was as if my family and my friend Eddie Hammer had vanished.

"Hammer?" I called again, louder.

A drip from the faucet plinked into the sink.

A thin, high-pitched hum pierced the silence. Though not loud, it was a clear, continuous beam of sound. It seemed to penetrate my eardrums, setting me on edge.

"Hammer!" I barked. "Quit fooling around!"

Still no answer. Just that irritating hum.

I glanced around the kitchen, then breathed a sigh of relief. I remember now. The refrigerator had started humming that new, high note whenever the motor came on. That probably meant the thing would break any day now.

Scolding myself for feeling so jumpy, I walked into the breakfast nook. I peered through the open door-way into the family room. The curtains were drawn to keep the room cool.

"Hammer!" My voice cracked. "Come and get it!"

A slim, dark form appeared out of the shadows.

I jumped.

"You feel it too, don't you?" the form whispered. "I can tell." The dark-haired figure in black clothes stepped into the light.

"Good grief, Hammer. Knock it off! Let's eat." My voice sounded too loud, even to me.

"You feel it too," Hammer repeated as he followed me to the kitchen. He looked nervously at the base-ment door. He even checked under his stool before he sat down at the bar. "Go on, Clint. Admit it."

Ever since I had moved with my family into our new home, Hammer had acted jumpy when he came over. He would only tell me that something about the house gave him the creeps. He never said what it was.

It's true that when we bought the old Lomer place, it was run down and looked kind of spooky.

But my folks had fixed it up. The rooms were light and airy now with lots of new modern fixtures.

That didn't matter to Hammer. He was still scared of the house. But whenever I pushed him for details about what bothered him, his responses were vague. "Something's just not right here," he would respond. "Can't you feel it?"

At first, I had shrugged off his suspicions and uneasiness about the place. Lately, however, Hammer's fear had begun to rub off on me. But I wasn't ready to admit that to him.

"The only thing I feel is you making me crazy," I told Hammer. I tore a gooey wedge from his side of the pizza.

Clink, slither, clink.

Hammer jumped a foot. The legs of his stool scraped across the floor. "Did you hear that? Something's coming up from the basement," he whispered.

We listened as the rubbing, clinking sound ascended the stairs. Then something rattled the knob on the basement door.

Hammer's fear got into me. I backed up against the kitchen counter. When I looked over at Hammer, he was as white as a sheet.

The doorknob turned. The basement door swung open with a low creak.

"Aahh!" cried Hammer. I felt my stomach drop.

3

"Hey, guys. What's going on?" My dad poked his head into the kitchen. I watched him pull the last three feet of garden hose up the stairs behind him. *Rub, clink, rub, clink.* The metal end knocked on each step as he reeled it in.

"Whew." Breath rushed out of Hammer. "Mr. Gleeson, it's you." He frowned. "Hey, Mr. G.? That's just . . . a hose, right?"

"Huh?" Dad shrugged. "Plain old garden hose." He pinched a few of its coils. "Same one we had at the old house. It kept uncoiling, so I just gave up and dragged it up behind me."

"Okay." Hammer smiled weakly. "But tell me something." The smile was gone now. "Why didn't we hear you walking up the stairs?"

"What?" Dad looked puzzled. Then he shrugged. "I guess the hose made so much noise you didn't hear me coming up."

"And I was calling you out here for pizza," I added as I pushed the pizza box toward my friend. "Dig in."

"Well, okay." Hammer reached into the box. He smiled a relieved smile, then he got that glimmer in his eyes. "Hey, Mr. G., I can give you a great deal on a slice of pizza. Extra toppings—just $1.75." Hammer picked pepperoni and olives from my half of the pizza and put them on the slice. Grinning, he held it out to my dad.

Dad set the coiled hose on the floor and joined us

at the kitchen bar. He pulled a dollar and change out of his pocket. "You're not a bad sales rep."

"Does that mean you're going to hire me at your computer store?" Hammer asked.

"We'll see—talk to me in a couple of years when you're old enough to hold a job." Dad smiled. Then he ate his pizza slice.

"Speaking of deals," he said as he wiped his lips on a napkin, "Clint, Mom and I made a decision. We're going to buy the property next door."

"Aarrgh!" Hammer gurgled through a mouthful of cheese.

Dad and I stared at him. We thought he was going to choke.

Hammer swallowed. But his eyes were wild. "You're going to buy the Haunted Swamp?"

"I beg your pardon?" said Dad.

"Isn't living next door to that place bad enough?" Hammer fairly shrieked. "No offense or anything. But don't you know what could be creeping into your basement? And now you want to buy . . . it? The Haunted Swamp?"

"What are you talking about?" My voice sounded shaky.

I had heard kids talk about the Haunted Swamp. But I'd never been sure where it was. Because I didn't want to look dumb, I'd never asked. Had Hammer just said it was the property next door?

"Snake ghosts slither through the reeds." Hammer made his voice spooky. His eyes opened to the size of headlights. "Go look. Twisty snake trails cover the swamp."

"Hammer," Dad said, placing a hand on my friend's shoulder, "you surprise me with that kind of talk. But it looks like you're really frightened."

Hammer nodded nervously.

"Hmm. You mind handing me that duct tape? . . . Thanks. Let me tell you something about fear. Sometimes it's healthy for you and sometimes it's not. Here, hold this." Dad pulled off a strip of tape, handed the roll to Hammer, and continued to talk as he wrapped a tiny hole in one end of the hose.

"Healthy fear is, say, a fear of being burned, so you don't touch a hot burner on the stove. Or a fear of getting cut, so you take precautions when you're using the lawn mower. Does that make sense?"

Hammer nodded again. "Yes, sir."

"Then there's unhealthy fear," Dad continued. "That's being afraid of things you can't do anything about, like thunder and lightning. Or being afraid of things that aren't real, like ghosts.

"Remember that Scripture the pastor talked about in his sermon on Sunday? Psalm 34:4? 'I asked the Lord for help, and he answered me. He saved me from all that I feared.' I expect if you seek the Lord in this, he'll help you out.

6

"There, that ought to do it," he said as he pressed the last of the tape into place. "I hope you'll think about that verse, Hammer."

Then Dad turned to me and asked, "Have you seen my pliers?"

"I think they're on the back porch," I answered.

"Thanks." He tousled Hammer's hair, then he reached for mine as he walked toward the door in search of his pliers.

"I think your dad must know everything in the whole world," Hammer said.

"He is pretty great, isn't he?" I said. I've got the best father around. Even though work keeps him pretty busy, he can always make time to talk about my problems or run baseball drills with me. And he teaches our Bible class at church.

"Who started that nonsense about the Haunted Swamp anyway?" I wondered.

"Who knows? But no matter what your father says, I wouldn't go into the Haunted Swamp for . . . even for a million dollars," Hammer declared.

I felt another chill race up my spine. Clearly, the property next door scared Hammer. Then I remembered what he'd said about something getting into the basement. Did he mean that ghosts could invade our home?

Suddenly I didn't feel hungry anymore. I set my slice of pizza on a plate and looked out the window at my dad, who was busy repairing something with his pliers.

I shivered.

Out of the corner of my eye I saw something move silently on the kitchen floor.

I drew in a startled breath and turned to stare. I stiffened when I saw the coiled shape on the floor behind Dad's stool.

Almost immediately I realized what I'd seen and exhaled slowly. Part of the garden hose had come uncoiled again. That was all.

I glanced at Hammer. Fortunately, he hadn't noticed my nervousness. He seemed to have relaxed some. He didn't even jump when Dad slammed the screen door on the way back inside.

"I'm going to remember what you said, Mr. G. But I thought you should know that land you want to buy is crawling with snake ghosts." Hammer gave my dad a worried look. "Maybe you better think about this some more."

Reasonably, my dad asked, "How do you know there are trails in there flattened by these so-called snake ghosts?"

"The whole town knows!" Hammer's tone was shrill. "Just go look. There's something creepy about the cabin on the property too. People who have dared to go into the swamp have seen lights flashing in the cabin's windows late at night."

"Probably just kids playing," Dad suggested. "And just to show you how gossip distorts the truth, that land isn't even swampy, yet it's called . . . what was the name?"

"The Haunted Swamp!"

"This may be Florida, but not all the land around here is swampy. And I wouldn't buy land that is," Dad pointed out.

He reached for his car keys.

"I've got to check on things down at the store, guys. Enjoy the rest of your lunch. And don't forget to clear the counter before your mom gets home, Clint."

"Okay, Dad."

After my dad left for work, I couldn't get my mind off the land next door.

"Hammer, if you knew that overgrown property next door was the Haunted Swamp, why didn't you tell me?" I asked.

"I thought you already knew," Hammer replied. "What did you think I was talking about when I asked you if you felt it too?"

"I didn't know! You never came straight out and told me what you were afraid of. I thought maybe you were spooked by this old house."

"I am! I mean, because it's so close to the swamp."

"Hammer, you heard what Dad said. The stories about the Haunted Swamp are just stories."

"I wish I could believe you, Clint. But I can't shake the eerie feeling I get when I'm here." Hammer checked his watch and said, "Hey, it's getting late. I told Mom I'd be home by now. Do you want to come over to my house this afternoon?"

"Okay . . . wait, no, I can't. I've got a baseball game today."

"Oh yeah. Good luck in your game. I'll call you later," Hammer said as he shut the front door behind him.

From the front window, I watched my friend pedal away on his bike. I wandered back to the kitchen and cleared off the counter. Then I walked into the family room.

Huge windows stood on each side of the fireplace. I went to the left one and stared out at the Haunted Swamp.

Next to our neatly mowed yard, the swamp reminded me of the messy kid's half of a shared bedroom. It was a jungle, bursting with green plant life. Long, thick vines hung like tentacles from the trees.

Tangled grasses and reeds, like reaching arms, crowded the edge of the lawn. They looked as if they might yank up bits of the yard while no one was looking.

A breeze fluttered the leaves. A second gust sent the grasses swaying.

It was just the wind. Wasn't it?

Maybe not all of the snakes were ghosts. Didn't I hear someone talking about live snakes in the grasses of the Haunted Swamp?

Some kids said the snake ghosts made the real snakes carry out their dirty work. Snakes supposedly slithered all over the property. They made so many trails that no one could ever get to know the lay of the land. Exploring in there, kids could get hopelessly lost.

I wondered if the snakes crossed the property line at night. They might slither across the lawn, inch by inch, coming closer, closer—

I'm getting as bad as Hammer! I clutched my head with both hands. I knew what I had to do to clear my mind. *Lord,* I prayed, *please deliver me from these fears. I know that in your presence I'm safe. Thank you.*

I took a deep breath. Then I made myself stare at the Haunted Swamp.

I carefully examined every clump of grass and spray of leaves I could see from the window. Left to

12

right. Right to left. Zigzag, up and down. I saw nothing out of the ordinary.

The place just looked overgrown with plants, that was all.

I had begun to relax and get my imagination under control.

Wham!

I jumped.

The garage door had banged open. Someone, or something, had entered the house.

Adrenaline surged through me. I looked around for something to protect myself with.

Before I could find anything, I heard a chirpy little voice say, "Hi, Clinty!"

My four-year-old sister, Kristin, bounded into the family room followed by my mother. Even though there are eight years between us, people often say Kristin and I look remarkably alike. We both have our father's blond hair, blue eyes, and freckles.

"Kristin, how many times have I asked you not to call me Clinty?" I said as Mom headed upstairs.

"I know a secret, Clinty," said Kristin, completely ignoring what I'd said.

"Good for you," I responded.

"The Three Bears are real!" Kristin blurted out.

"That's nice," I said.

"They are! Goldilocks's Three Bears. I saw them. I know where they live."

"Where's that?" I asked, even though I really wasn't interested.

"They live in the cabin," sang Kristin. "The cabin in the jungle place next to our house."

I swung around. My eyes locked on Kristin. She had my full attention now. "Show me," I demanded.

We clattered out the front door, Kristin in the lead. When Mom heard the front door slam, she called, "Clint! Don't leave the house!"

I jerked to a stop and looked up. Mom had yelled from the balcony off her bedroom.

She leaned over the railing, gripping it hard. Strands of reddish hair blew into her eyes. Her face was crinkled with worry.

"What's wrong, Mom?" I cried. Had she seen something creepy from an upstairs window? Something in the swamp?

"Did you forget you have a game this afternoon? I can't believe you don't have your uniform on yet."

"Oohh." I let out the breath I didn't realize I'd been holding. "I got distracted by Kristin."

"Well, you had better change and get going. Kristin and I will walk over to the ballpark in a few minutes." Mom went back inside and shut the balcony doors behind her.

I dashed up to my room. After I pulled on my Little League uniform, I grabbed my glove and cleats and hurried back downstairs. Outside I quickly put on my cleats and raced to the ballpark.

Good thing we live so close, I thought as I ran.

Part of the ballpark also bordered the Haunted Swamp. When our team was batting, I couldn't see the swamp. But when I played first base, I could see it very well. And since the other team was very good, I had a lot of time to look at it.

From first base, the Haunted Swamp looked huge.

From the family room window I had only been able to see a small part of it. But now that I was outdoors, and I knew what supposedly lurked there, the swamp seemed to spread out for miles.

Grass and reeds grew so tall that I couldn't see the trunks of some of the trees. But their branches were visible, the foliage so lush that it covered the property like a canopy. I wondered how dark it would be beneath those branches.

"Safe!"

"Get in the game, Clint!" yelled Coach Wagner.

I blushed. I should have gotten this guy out easily. We lost, six to five.

"So close," I moaned as I walked home with Mom and Kristin. "I'm glad Dad missed this game."

Mom kept Kristin occupied as I thought about how I'd played. No one had blamed me for the loss. Still, I knew we could have won if I'd gotten a couple more outs.

That's it, Lord, I prayed. *Now I'm letting others down because of my fears. I can't let some silly swamp throw my game. I'm going over there right after sup-per. With your guidance, I'll prove to myself there are no ghosts in there.*

At home, I changed my clothes and then ran back downstairs.

"Is Dad home yet?" I asked as I set the table for dinner.

"No, the store's open late tonight," Mom answered.

My parents owned and operated a computer store. They took turns working shifts so that one of them could be home with me and Kristin.

We sat down together, and I choked down two meatballs, three forkfuls of salad, and four swallows of milk.

"May I be excused?" I asked. "I'm not very hungry."

Mom raised her eyebrows at me—I'm always hungry. But she excused me from the table with a shrug. I ran through the garage and out of the house. I looked toward the sun in the western sky. I figured I still had plenty of daylight to explore.

"Clinty! Wait for me," squeaked a high voice behind me.

"Kristin, you stay home," I said.

"I want to see the Three Bears. And I can tell you about them. Nobody else can."

"Oh, all right," I agreed. "Hurry up. But keep your voice down."

"The Three Bears are big," chattered Kristin.

We walked into the jungle next door. When my shoes hit the thick, matted grass, I felt as though I were walking in slow motion. It was like walking in water.

Or maybe quicksand.

I grimaced as I stepped high. Tall weeds flicked at my legs as I pushed my way through. I shuddered at the thought of a snake ghost coiling around my ankles.

"The bears were sitting in their chairs," babbled Kristin. "But they didn't move at all. I think it was just time for sitting."

"Hold it." I stopped still. I thought I'd heard something.

Swish, sssss. There it was! A sound like something was crawling through the high grass. Or to be more exact, slithering through the grass.

Sssssssss.

My heart skipped a beat.

Sss. Sss. Sss. The sound grew fainter. Whatever made the sound had moved farther away from us. Beads of sweat broke out on my forehead and began to roll down my face.

"Come on!" Kristin demanded.

I gulped and started forward again. Then I remembered something. "Kristin. Did you say chairs?" I asked.

"Yup. Chairs," she answered.

"In the cabin?"

"Of course, in the cabin." Kristin looked irritated that I hadn't paid close attention the first time.

"Did you play Goldilocks and go in?" *Keep talking, Clint,* I thought. *Forget snake ghosts.*

"'Course not. For Goldilocks to go in, the bears have to not be home," she said.

"Where is the cabin, anyway?" I asked.

"Behind the jail tree." Kristin pointed.

I looked at the tree. Thick, twisted vines hung from its branches, all the way to the ground. I thought there had to be at least a hundred of them. The vines did look like the bars of a jail.

Or like a hundred dangling snakes.

I winced at that last thought. I raised my gaze to the branches and leaves. They were so wide and thick a city could be built on top of them.

"Besides," Kristin said, "it was locked."

I slowly groped my way back to our conversation. "The cabin door was locked?" I asked.

"Yup."

We walked around the jail tree. The ground dipped down for a short distance and then rose up again. When we reached the top of a little hill, I could see the cabin below. Kristin scampered right toward it. I had trouble making my feet move.

The cabin looked charred from a long-past fire, yet it seemed sturdy. I shivered. How could wood look so blackened and remain so sturdy?

The cabin contrasted with its surroundings. It was the only thing made by human hands in that whole green mass of twisted vines. Who had lived here? And if this was an abandoned cabin, why was the door locked?

I watched Kristin jump up on a rock to look in a window. Then I forced myself to walk down the hill toward her.

When I reached the cabin, I pressed my face to the dirty window too. I had no idea what I would see.

As I struggled to make out the cabin's interior, my concentration was broken—by the piercing sound of Kristin's shriek.

"Kristin!" My right ear throbbed from the blast of her voice. "What's wrong? Why did you scream?"

Wildly, I checked for snakes clutching Kristin's arms, legs, or hair. None.

Then I jerked around and scanned the grass behind us. Nothing again. But why would I have to see anything? Snake ghosts would be invisible, wouldn't they?! They could be anywhere. I tried to control my rising fear.

"It's really, really real," Kristin chattered, happily. She still had her face pressed against the window, her nose pushed flat against the pane.

"Huh? What's real?" I twisted back toward the window. After rubbing my fists on the grimy glass, I looked inside again. "I can't see a thing in there." Was Kristin just playing a game of pretend?

"That's 'cause they're gone," Kristin cried. "They went for their walk. They even put their chairs away. The Three Bears are real!"

I stared at my sister. Her pale blue eyes were as round as marbles. Her small cheeks were so flushed I couldn't see her freckles.

Kristin must have seen something here. Something that looked like three bears. She wouldn't get this excited over a game of pretend.

"Mom and Dad think the Three Bears are just make-believe." A happy smile filled Kristin's face. "But they're not. They're real."

I peered hard through the window. I could see another window straight across the cabin and one in the back wall. As I got accustomed to the faint light, I could see that the place was empty. At least there weren't any bears or chairs inside.

"Maybe it's 'chanted," sang Kristin.

"Chanted?" I asked. Through the window, I stared left, then right, as far as I could. I couldn't see a hint of color. The whole inside looked as sooty and dark as the outside. What did she mean by chanted?

"The whole place is 'chanted. It's the 'chanted forest." Kristin's voice fell to a whisper. "Or else the bears couldn't go out of the cabin and walk in it."

Oh, the enchanted forest. I looked at Kristin once more. I was about to tell her she couldn't possibly have seen the Three Bears but thought better of it. Why spoil her fun?

"Hey, Kristin, I'm going to look in the other window. You can come with me if you want. In fact—" I looked around at the tangled mass of green surrounding us.

"Come anyway." I grabbed Kristin's arm and walked around to the back of the cabin.

This window was just as dirty as the first. It was dotted with water spots and larger splashes of dried mud. I cupped my hands around my eyes and gazed inside. I tried not to breathe in the powdery dirt.

Again, the floors and walls looked black and shadowy. Going in there would be like stepping from day into night. I wondered if this was the ghosts' dark resting place. Ugghhh. I didn't want to think about that.

I was about to step away from the window. Then, out of the corner of my eye, I saw a shape hulking in a far corner of the cabin. My stomach lurched.

Kristin tugged at my elbow. "You go away now, Clinty. Goldilocks has to go in alone."

"What?" I shook her off my arm. Then what she had said sank in. I whirled to face her and said, "Hey, no way are you going in there. You stay out here!"

I swallowed and looked back at the shape again. It rose about a third of the way up the cabin wall. Though bulky all over, it looked thinner on top than at the bottom. It didn't move.

Was it just the very darkest pocket of dark in the cabin? Was it where the snake ghosts' slept? Was it—

"You go now, Clinty," Kristin pleaded, trying to push me away. "There are no boys in the story. Goldilocks has to go in all by herself."

I remembered that Kristin had said the cabin door

25

was locked. I had no plans to try the door, though, or to let Kristin try it.

I stepped back from the window and looked all around its edges. I didn't think it would open. At least not from the outside. My stomach unclenched a bit. Kristin probably couldn't get inside the cabin.

"Clinty—"

"Sshh! Kristin, listen." I swung my sister up on my shoulders. "Look in there. In the corner on the left." I wiggled Kristin's left arm. "This is left. Is that one of the bears?"

I heard a gentle bump as Kristin pressed her forehead against the glass. "That big lump? 'Course not. The bears are real bears. I saw them!"

I sighed. If Kristin wasn't frightened, then I certainly shouldn't be either.

An instant later, terror returned.

Something had crept up behind us.

It curled around my ankles.

I forced myself not to scream.

I couldn't bend my neck to look down at my feet. Then I realized the thing weaving between my ankles felt like fur, not snake skin. Could the snake ghosts change form? My neck strained backward as Kristin's weight sagged down on my shoulders. The legs of Kristin's jeans rubbed hard on my skin.

Had the furry creature reached up to pull Kristin off my shoulders?

"Clinty! Clinteeeey!"

I clung to Kristin's wrists and staggered, fighting for balance. If I fell now, we'd both land right in the furry thing's clutches.

Or tumble straight down its throat.

Kristin locked her ankles around my neck. I felt panic quiver through me.

But the furry thing had gone.

In the distance, I heard, "Rrreeouw. Rrreeouw."

"Kristin!" I rasped. "What is that?" It certainly wasn't the roar of a bear.

"A kitty! It was a kitty. But you scared it away. Clinty, I want down."

Before I could respond, Kristin unhooked her feet. I gulped a huge breath. She wormed her way over my shoulder and squirmed down to my hip. Then she dropped easily to the ground.

"A cat?" I asked. I rubbed my neck gingerly. "Did you see it?"

"Sure. It was black with big yellow eyes. All black. But I can't think of a story with a black kitty in it."

A cat, I thought. *A visible cat. A visible black cat. Not a ghost. But where had it come from?*

"Hey, Kristin," I said, "are you sure ... there wasn't something ... pulling you off me?" I felt silly asking. I sounded as paranoid as Hammer.

Kristin cocked her head at me. "Pulling me? 'Course not. Nobody pulls on Goldilocks in the story. I just wanted down."

I sighed.

In the dense forest I couldn't see the sun. But it must have been setting low in the western sky. It was getting darker. I didn't want to get lost in this place when the sun set.

"Come on, Kristin. We've got to go home. It's close to your bedtime." I leaned over to scoop Kristin into my arms.

"No!" Kristin screeched. She churned her arms and legs, trying to struggle free.

"Cut it out," I puffed. I winced as she kicked and fought me. Still, I held on.

"You go home!" Kristin cried. "I'm Goldilocks, and I want to stay here."

I gasped and almost dropped her as she continued to struggle. It was as if she were under a spell. She really believed she was Goldilocks!

"You're not in the storyyyyyy!" Kristin cried.

I was in no mood to get kicked again. "Fine!" I said as I let go of my sister. I turned and stamped through the grass toward home. I'd send Mom back to collect Kristin.

If there are any snakes in my way, I'll crush them to dust, I thought. *I'll . . . I'll . . .* But I couldn't think what else I'd do. My stomach churned with fear again.

What if the snake ghosts know I'm on my way to get Mom? They'd also know she would rescue Kristin from them. And they'd blame me. Their fangs would rise from the reeds and—

I broke into a run, swishing loudly through the high grass. That way I'd never hear the snake sounds.

When I reached the jail tree, I ran wide around it. I didn't want one of those long, twisted tentacles to reach out and grab me.

The ghosts had let Kristin into their story games. But not me. I was too old to play their games. They probably resented me for it, and they would try to get me. After all, I was on their land.

I pumped my legs as fast as I could. But I didn't seem to be getting anywhere.

Where was my yard? This grass tugging at my shoes, the vines yanking at my hair, they had to end sometime. I didn't remember going so far into the swamp. Had it grown bigger?

Finally I spied my house. I lurched onto my lawn and dropped to my knees in relief. But my relief lasted only a second.

The black cat crept from behind the trunk of a palm tree. It stalked to the center of the yard, then turned to stare at me. Its ribs rippled like a Slinky toy. Its gold eyes glowed like lamps. It showed no fear.

The cat obviously isn't afraid of whatever's in the swamp, I thought.

I forced myself to calm down and waited until my breathing returned to normal. I was just about to get up and tell Mom that Kristin was still in the swamp when something rustled the tall weeds behind me. I sprang to my feet.

"Who's there?!" I yelled. My voice cracked. My fear had returned.

The only answer was the continuing rustle of the plants.

The sound grew louder.

I looked at the tall grass bordering the yard. Something was parting the grass—something low to the ground.

And it was coming straight toward me.

I turned and sprinted toward the house. When I was halfway to the front door, I heard, "Clinty!"

Gasping for breath, I looked back toward the swamp. And saw Kristin standing at the edge of the yard. Abruptly I sat down.

For the first time I noticed that the weeds towered over Kristin. She had parted the grass as she ran toward home. But she had been hidden by the tall growth.

As she walked over to me, I asked, slightly annoyed, "Kristin, why didn't you answer when I called?"

"Huh?" Kristin looked puzzled.

"Never mind." I was too tired to press her. I guessed she just didn't hear me.

"It started getting too dark. I didn't want to play anymore," she said simply.

Maybe Kristin hadn't been under a spell after all. Maybe she'd just been caught up in her own imagination.

The porch light came on. "What are you kids doing out there?" Mom called from the door. She stepped out of the house and looked at me. "Clint, what's wrong? Why are you just sitting in the middle of the lawn?"

"We were just playing, Mom. I guess I was running too hard and needed a rest. I'm okay."

"Kristin, it's almost your bedtime. You had better come in. After you wash your face and brush your teeth, I'll read you a bedtime story," Mom said.

"I want to hear the story of Goldilocks and the Three Bears," Kristin announced with a grin.

I groaned and pulled myself off the grass.

As we walked to the house, Kristin spotted the cat.

"Kitty!" Kristin exclaimed. "Here, kitty."

In all the excitement, I had forgotten about the cat.

"Kristin, leave that cat alone!" I said. "It might hurt you."

"Clint, it's just a cat," Mom said. "And it's a very gentle one. I've seen it around several times since we moved."

"Nice kitty." Kristin tenderly stroked the cat's back.

"You've seen this cat before?" I asked.

"Almost every morning when I walk out to get the paper," Mom answered. "I think it belongs to a family down the road."

"Oh." I felt silly for thinking the cat was a messenger from the snake ghosts. So far, I hadn't done a good job of taking my father's advice and overcoming my fears.

"Kristin, you can pet the kitty another time. Let's get you ready for bed," Mom said.

I followed Kristin into the house where I headed straight for the telephone in the family room. I had to tell Hammer about my adventure.

"You went in there?!" Hammer asked so loudly that I had to hold the receiver away from my ear.

"I had to check it out, Hammer. I mean, if Mom and Dad are going to buy the place, well—"

But Hammer cut me off: "I can't believe it! Don't you realize the danger you put yourself in?"

"Don't you think you're overreacting, Hammer?" I asked. "I admit, it was pretty spooky. It's so dark in there. But Kristin thought the swamp was a great place to play pretend."

"You took your little sister with you?" Hammer cried.

"She's been in there before. Alone! She thinks the Three Bears live in there. She even showed me the cabin where she thinks the bears live," I explained.

"Oh, man, you went to the cabin?" Hammer's voice leaped across the telephone line.

"Yeah. I even looked in the windows. It was pretty dark in there. There was something hanging out in the corner of the cabin. Something big."

"What was it?"

"I don't know. It was too dark to tell. But Kristin saw it, and she wasn't afraid of it. In fact, Kristin thought we were in an enchanted forest. She was really acting strange for a while."

"Strange? What do you mean?" Hammer asked.

"I mean she was so absorbed in her make-believe game. It kind of scared me. It was like she was under a spell or something," I explained.

"You could be right. I've heard stories about the snake ghosts putting spells on animals and even people. That's how they get them to carry out their orders," Hammer said.

I sat silent for a minute. The thought of my sister being under the spell of the snake ghosts made me shiver.

Finally, I said, "Listen, Hammer, this has got to stop. It's one thing to be a little bit nervous, but it's something else to say my sister's under a spell. I can't imagine the Lord would be too happy with us for even thinking such things.

"I've got an idea," I continued. "Meet me here tomorrow morning. If something real is threatening my sister, I want to get to the bottom of it."

"What's your idea?" Hammer asked.

"Just meet me here tomorrow. We're going in there together."

"Into the Haunted Swamp?" my friend gasped.

"Listen, Gleeson, I don't think that's a good idea."

"Hammer, if there's really something in there, it's only a matter of time before it comes after me and my parents . . . and eventually the whole town. But if Dad's right, and there aren't any snake ghosts, then we have nothing to be afraid of. Maybe we'll even find some simple explanation for the rumors."

"I'm still not sure about this . . ." Hammer paused. "But, okay, I'll show up tomorrow morning."

That night in bed, I had a heart-to-heart talk with the heavenly Father: "I know that you are always with me, and I'm counting on you to deliver me from my fears. Please keep us safe tomorrow and help us figure out what's going on in that swamp. Good night, Lord."

I drifted off to a peaceful sleep. But I hadn't been asleep long when something jolted me awake. My eyelids flew open. My heart was pounding. I sat up in bed and looked around the room.

What had awakened me?

A sudden flash of light momentarily illuminated the bedroom. I gasped.

In that momentary flash of light I had seen a figure standing in the doorway.

BOOM!

Thunder sounded only seconds after the lightning flash. It seemed to shake the house.

At the same moment, something jumped onto my bed.

I couldn't help myself; I let out a shriek.

"I'm scared, Clinty!" Kristin wailed as she grabbed my arm.

When I recognized her voice, I shook off my fear. "Me too," I managed to say to comfort her. "That thunder's pretty loud. But we're safe in the house."

"Clint!" my mom said from the doorway. "Are you okay? I could hear you all the way down the hall."

"Yes, Mom, I'm okay. Kristin just startled me."

"Mommy, Mommy!" Kristin cried as she ran toward Mom.

"I know, sweetie. The storm's scary, isn't it?" Mom picked up my sister and stroked her hair. Kristin clung tightly to Mom's neck.

"Remember what I told you about thunder, honey?" she asked as she sat down on the end of my bed, still holding Kristin close. "It's just God whispering."

"But he whispers so loud!" Kristin's voice sounded muffled against Mom's robe.

"Yes, he does. You're right. And he sounds like he could hurt us, but he won't because he loves us."

Kristin peeked up at Mom questioningly.

"Yes, it's true," Mom said. "He loves you, Kristin, and I do too."

Another loud peal sounded from the sky.

"Somebody's frightened by the storm, I see," Dad said from the doorway. "Kristin, my girl, have you forgotten what thunder is?"

"God whispering!" we all answered, then laughed. Mom and Dad had told us that about thunder for as long as I could remember.

"Some friends and I were talking about thunder at school a couple of days ago," I told them. "We all had different explanations for it that we'd grown up with.

"One girl said her parents told her God was moving furniture."

My parents laughed, and Kristin again peeked out from the collar of Mom's robe.

"Someone else said he'd heard it was God bowling," I continued.

"I've heard that one too," Dad commented. "Your Grandfather Gleeson always told me the clouds were just bumping into each other. But I couldn't figure that one out. Clouds looked so soft and thunder sounded so hard!"

That drew an outright laugh from Kristin. "Clouds are so soft and thunder's so hard! You're funny, Daddy."

"Well, I'm glad you think so, princess," Dad said, swinging her up into his arms. "Do you also think you could get back to sleep? Kiss your brother good night. Morning will be here before you know it."

And it was. I must have dropped right off to sleep because next thing I knew, sunlight streamed through my bedroom window.

Hammer knocked on our back door and let himself in just as I finished breakfast.

"Hey. Some storm last night, huh?" Hammer sat down across from me at the breakfast table.

"I'll say. It sounded like it was right over the house," I answered.

"The ground's pretty soggy this morning," Hammer added as I cleared my dishes from the table. While I put them in the dishwasher, Mom bustled in with Kristin.

"Oh, good morning, Eddie," she greeted my friend. Then she turned to me and said, "Clint, I'm going to take Kristin to run some errands now. I'll see you later."

"Okay, Mom. See you."

After she left, Hammer looked at me and wrinkled his brow questioningly. "So what's the plan?"

"To find out the truth about the Haunted Swamp," I answered. "Come on. Let's get going."

We walked to the edge of my yard.

"Is this where you and Kristin went in yesterday?" Hammer asked.

"This is it. Are you ready?"

"Clint, I don't know. Maybe we better think about this some more," my friend said, hesitating at the edge of the swamp.

"Don't back out on me now, Hammer. I need your help in this," I pleaded.

Hammer looked directly into my eyes and took a deep breath. "Okay. Here we go."

We stepped into the tall, weedy grass. The ground beneath our feet was soggy.

"This really is a swamp!" Hammer said.

"It wasn't like this yesterday. The rain really soaked the ground."

"The ground's not the only thing that's soaked. Look at my shoes," Hammer complained as he pointed to his feet. "Why do your parents want to buy this place anyway?"

"I don't know," I said, ducking under a low fan of leaves. "But if they do buy it, maybe they'll clear out some of this dense brush."

"Look. The grass is flat there, and there, and there." Hammer pointed as he spoke. "Just like everybody says."

Oh boy. Hammer would get going on snakes immediately. I didn't want to get spooked.

"Sure, parts of the grass are flattened," I reassured him. "Kristin and I walked on it yesterday."

We walked in tense silence for a few minutes.

"Aagh!" Hammer suddenly screamed.

I jerked back. "What?!" My voice sounded shrill from fear. "What's wrong?"

Hammer pointed straight ahead. "Look at that thing!"

I looked past his finger and saw the tree. "Kristin calls that the jail tree," I said with relief in my voice. "It's perfectly safe."

"Look at all those vines!" Hammer said in wonder. He had stopped about ten feet from the jail tree. "There must be hundreds of them. And look at the ones coiled around those branches." Hammer pointed up. "They look like—"

"Like snakes," I said. "I know."

"Do you think maybe the snakes aren't invisible after all?" Hammer asked.

I didn't want to tell Hammer that I'd had that thought.

Who knew what lived among those vines and branches? Surely snakes could. They just might slither down those thick vines and coil around trespassers like us.

I looked up. A thick mat of leaves blotted out the sun.

I eyed the vines hanging from the branches as we wound our way around the tree. They looked strong enough to swing on.

"You know, I saw an old Tarzan movie once on TV," Hammer said. "Tarzan swung from tree to tree on vines like these."

"I've seen some of those old movies too." I grabbed one of the vines and tugged on it. It held strong to the branch above. "Well, there's no reason why we can't have a little fun on this ghost-busting mission."

"What are you doing, Gleeson?" Hammer's voice was wary.

Gripping the vine with both hands, I backed up as far as the vine would let me. Then I ran full speed straight ahead and lifted my feet off the ground.

"Whoopeeeee!" I shouted as I swung into the air.

But my excitement quickly changed into something like fear. The vine swung me higher than I had expected.

"Gleeson! Let go of the vine!" Hammer yelled.

The vine began to swing back toward where I'd started. I held on tightly as I picked up speed. If I let go now, I could get seriously hurt.

As the vine continued to swing me around, it no longer felt like a plant. It felt more like a long, strong muscle. It was toying with me, lifting me higher and higher.

I caught a glimpse of Hammer's panic-stricken face. I could see I was definitely in some kind of danger.

Maybe this isn't a vine after all, I thought.

"Let go, Gleeson!" Hammer shrieked.

On my next swing back toward the ground, I let go of the vine. I landed inside the jail tree's ring of vines. Looking around, I realized this made a pretty good hiding place. If the swamp weren't so spooky, I wouldn't mind a hideaway like this.

"Man," Hammer puffed. He moved slowly toward me. "I thought you were done for. I thought one of the snake ghosts had taken control of the vine."

Hammer shuffled closer. He held out a hand. "Hey, Clint? You okay? You didn't break any bones, did you?"

"Nah," I croaked. I clasped Hammer's hand and hauled myself to my feet. Then I looked at my hands. They were covered with green plant stains. It had been nothing but a vine after all.

I went back to the vine and gave it a push. It swayed gently. I forced strength into my voice. "A vine."

"What?" Hammer didn't catch what I'd said.

"Never mind. Check this place out, Hammer. It's kind of cool. You can almost hide in here."

45

Hammer looked around the dark enclosure.

"I see what you mean. But I don't think it's cool. I think it's creepy. Come on, let's get to the cabin and get this over with."

"Hold it, Hammer! Look!"

"Yikes!" said Hammer when he saw my discovery. The soft, mossy mound we were standing next to was only camouflage. We had found the door to a tunnel.

"Come on, let's go in," I said, putting my hand on the entrance to the tunnel.

"What? Are you out of your mind? You can't go in there! And you certainly can't open that door. Do you want the snake ghosts to know we've discovered their passageway?"

What Hammer said made sense. I wasn't convinced we were dealing with ghosts, but we still could cause some serious trouble by opening the door. Whoever or whatever used this tunnel didn't need to know we'd found it.

"Where do you suppose it leads?" I wondered.

"My theory is that it leads all over town. Of course, it depends how far the ghosts want to go."

"Maybe you're right, Hammer. But since when do *ghosts* need tunnels to move around? They can be invisible if they want," I observed.

"That may be true," Hammer said, "but the ghosts may need a place where they can drag their . . . victims."

We both shuddered. Suddenly the hideaway didn't seem remotely cozy.

"Come on, we've found what you were looking for, haven't we? Let's go," Hammer said.

"Not yet. This just raises more questions. The cabin is only a short way from here. Let's keep going," I answered.

We walked through more clumps of weeds and grass.

"Cut around to the right," I said.

I hadn't meant to speak so softly . . . as if I were afraid something would hear me.

We crept around the jail tree. I thought we'd never get to the other side. Was the jail tree spreading too? Just like the whole swamp seemed to be?

At last we made it to the top of the little hill and peered down at the cabin.

The roof looked much steeper than I remembered. It seemed to point toward the sky, making the cabin look like a ghostly rocket.

"Three Bears' house, huh?" Hammer's voice made me jump. "They must have painted it with coal tar. Look how dark it is."

"Come on." I started down the hill before I could lose my nerve. Hammer stayed at my side.

"Here's the first window I looked in," I told my friend. "Kristin claims she saw bears sitting on chairs in here."

"What?" Hammer said. "You're kidding, right?"

We cupped our hands around our eyes and pressed our faces to the window. Immediately I felt dust creep up my nose. I stepped back from the window and sneezed.

That same instant Hammer let out a yelp.

Hammer jumped away from the window. He almost knocked me over.

"What's wrong?" I yelled.

Hammer pointed to the window. "F-frogs!"

"Frogs?" I asked. "What's so scary about frogs?" Hammer had never been afraid of them before.

I leaned my forehead against the window and peered inside. Then I saw them.

Frogs! The cabin floor was covered with them. Masses of them, leaping, jiggling, scrambling all over one another.

How did they just appear overnight? We hadn't seen any frogs outside the cabin.

"Gleeson! Come on!" Hammer yelled over his shoulder. He was already running away from the cabin.

I tore myself away from the window and bolted up the hill after my friend. We stumbled and grabbed at green plants to pull ourselves along. Then we flew around the jail tree.

I felt a cramp in my side. I could hear Hammer wheezing ahead of me. How much farther would we have to run? It seemed like the Haunted Swamp would never end.

Suddenly something snagged Hammer's left ankle. He fell forward and caught himself with his arms.

Whatever had snagged him pulled tight. As he struggled to get free, he rolled over and looked at his ankle.

"Snake!" he cried.

The hair on the back of my neck stood up.

I stared at Hammer. Fear tightened my chest, making it hard to breathe.

"Help me!" Hammer yelled. "A snake's got me!"

Hammer was panicking. Flailing his arms and screaming, he continued to pull against the thing at his ankle.

"I'll help you!" I shouted as I neared my friend.

I grabbed a stick to knock the snake away from Hammer. But when I got close enough to see his ankle, a rush of relief washed over me.

"Hammer, your ankle is caught in a tree root. It's not a snake," I told him.

Hammer was still panicked. It took a few seconds for him to grasp what I had said.

By the time he looked down at his ankle again, I had pulled out my pocketknife. I steadily sawed away at the tree root to free him.

"Just about got it. There. You're free," I said as I stood up, folded the blade, and put the knife back into my pocket.

Hammer bent down and massaged his ankle with his hand. The root had scraped the skin when he had tried to struggle free.

Hammer's heart was still pounding. He took a deep breath. "I thought I was a goner," he said.

"I know how you feel," I said. "When I was swinging on that vine earlier, I thought it was a snake too," I admitted. "It's this place . . . It's creepy."

Hammer tried to walk but limped on his sore ankle.

"I don't think I can run on this. You go ahead. I'll have to walk out of here," he told me.

"No way," I said. "If you have to walk, then I'll walk too."

As we made our way slowly out of the swamp, something kept bothering me.

"You know," I said, "I don't understand how those frogs got in the cabin. They weren't there yesterday."

"When you looked in the cabin yesterday, did you see the floor?" Hammer asked, "I mean, clearly?"

I thought for a second before I answered, "No. It was pretty dark. I could just make out shadows."

"Do you suppose there's a big hole in the floor? Maybe the tunnel leads there. Maybe the frogs get in and out that way."

"I suppose that could be," I said. "That would be an explanation."

Hammer stopped walking. "Don't you know what a hole in the cabin floor means?"

52

"No. What?" I stopped and looked at my friend.

"Where do ghosts come from anyway?" he asked.

I wondered what he was getting at.

Hammer continued. "They come from . . . under the ground where animals are buried—don't they?" He started walking again. His ankle had started to feel better. "So they have to come out of a hole in the earth. That's why they have their house right on top of it. And the tunnel you found is part of their network."

"Aw, Hammer, that's got to be the most ridicu—"

Sssssss. The sound came from behind us.

"What was that?" Hammer cried.

Ssssssss.

"Run!" I screamed.

My heart pounded. It had to be a snake. And it sounded close.

"Heeheehee, hehheh, hawhawhaw." A high-pitched, chilling cackle of a laugh echoed behind us.

Not a snake. That was not a snake. Not an animal. My thoughts raced. It was either a human, or a—

Ghost!

Grass, weeds, and more grass. Where was my front yard? I began to believe that we would never get out of the Haunted Swamp. We could be trapped in here forever with the snake ghosts!

"Your house!" Hammer yelled. "Up ahead."

We broke through the tall, reedy grass and

broad-jumped onto my lawn. We lay there trembling and gasping.

I felt as if we had leaped onto a lifeboat—one that had been drifting away from us. It was several minutes before either of us spoke.

"You've got to tell your parents about what we saw and heard." Hammer's voice was weak. "I mean, I'm not going in there again, so I'm okay. But for your sake, man. And Kristin's. They've got to believe you."

I shook my head. "They probably walked all over that property before they decided to buy it. Clearly they didn't see or hear anything unusual. They might think I'm imagining things.

"But those frogs, the door into the ground, that horrible laugh—we know that something or someone is in the Haunted Swamp."

"Hey, Clint," Hammer whispered. "Look what's coming."

I lifted my head and saw Kristin walking toward us. She was wearing some of her dress-up clothes. Her long white dress trailed on the ground behind her. Her blond hair was brushed out loose. A gold, glittery circle sat on her head like a crown.

The strangest thing was the *way* she was walking. So slowly, like she was in a trance.

She headed toward the swamp.

"Kristin?" I heard the catch in my voice. "Where are you going?"

"They called me," she said simply.

"Huh? Who called you?" Hammer asked.

Kristin turned to face him. "The bears in the forest. They need me. They called me. Didn't you hear them?"

She turned away from us and walked into the swamp.

Stunned, I watched my sister disappear into the swamp. After a few seconds I realized I had to go back in there. I had to rescue my sister.

I rushed into the tall weeds yelling, "Kristin!"

I caught sight of her white dress. The skirt was caught on a low bush.

I lunged for her, intending to break the spell and pull her to safety.

Color rose in Kristin's face. Her forehead creased with anger.

She jammed her hands on her hips and yelled, "You spoiled it!" She stamped her foot. "Boys are not in the story!" She stomped back toward the house.

I felt shaken by her outburst. Kristin had never been so angry at me.

"Good job, man," Hammer said as I crept out of the swamp. He still lay sprawled on the ground.

"I thought there was a spell on her," I said as I stared toward the house.

"Probably was. You broke it. Good job," he said again.

I shook my head. It was time to get hold of myself. "We've got to be imagining things, Hammer," I said.

"What about the hissing noise? What about the laugh? I know we both heard those," he pointed out.

"Probably just kids goofing around," I said.

I looked at Hammer and added, "What if it's kids from our class? They're probably falling all over each other laughing at how they scared us."

"I don't know." Hammer got to his feet and walked to his bike. "I hope you're right. But remember one thing. Those frogs we saw were real. So was the door to the tunnel."

As I watched Hammer pedal down the street, my stomach growled. I hadn't realized how hungry I was.

When I went inside I discovered Dad was home.

"Lunch isn't quite ready yet," he said. "Kristin's playing in her room until it's made. She seemed kind of mad when she came inside. Is everything okay?"

I nodded silently. I wasn't ready to tell him about the snake ghosts yet. I was glad he didn't press me for details. Instead, he seemed to be thinking about something else.

After a moment he said, "Will you do me a favor? In the basement, there are a bunch of shelves. Somewhere I know I have a can of WD–40. See if you can find it, okay? I want to oil the squeaky hinge on the basement door after lunch."

"Sure, Dad," I said with a smile.

I opened the basement door. *Creeeak.*

"See what I mean?" Dad asked.

I looked down the steps. It was like looking down a black tunnel. It was so much darker than the sunny kitchen.

The steps were steep. My shoes clumped down them loudly. About halfway down, I smelled a damp, musty odor. It grew even stronger when I reached the concrete floor. Where was the light switch?

I ran my fingers over the chilly wall. I jumped back when a sharp needle of pain pricked under my nail.

"Ouch!"

Cautiously I felt along the wall again for the light switch. I felt a very rough, jagged piece of wall. That must be what stabbed my finger.

My eyes had begun to adjust to the darkness. I gave up on finding the switch and struck out to find the shelves without the light. *Let's see,* I thought, *they're somewhere to the right. Then straight back to the corner.*

As I began walking, I felt cobwebs brush my face. A spider dropped onto my hand and scurried across my arm. I flinched and brushed it away, but stifled the instinct to cry out. I didn't want Dad to think I was afraid.

I had only gone a few steps when a rushing, whirring sound began. I gasped. Air began to blow, and a string bounced off my forehead. I grabbed it with both hands and pulled. There was a scraping sound, and the light came on. The chain clinked against the bulb when I let go of the string attached to it.

I looked behind me. The whirring sound came from the dehumidifier. Its motor hummed. Water plinked into its tray. Mom had plugged it in to make the basement less damp. She hoped the basement would smell better once it dried out.

I turned and squared my shoulders. The storage shelves weren't far ahead.

As I walked, I noticed how rough the gray ceiling was. It looked like gobs of rumpled tissue. Dust danced in the light. My sneeze exploded in my ears.

I reached the far corner where the storage shelves were. But the corner was pretty dark. Without enough light, I couldn't make out the hulking objects on the shelves.

I scanned the ceiling. After a moment, I found the small pear shape hanging down from the ceiling. I groped for the chain that would turn the light on.

Click. Light flooded the area.

A piece of green garden hose looped down from one of the shelves.

As I watched, it slowly moved onto the shelf and disappeared behind a box.

My heart thudded against my chest.

"Snake!" I screamed.

Hammer had guessed right.

The snake ghosts could get into the basement. This snake was as green as the grass in the Haunted Swamp.

I knew what was happening. The snakes were closing in on my house.

The reptile's knobby head poked around the box.

I took a step backward, watching the slithering serpent carefully.

"Clint?" Dad's silhouette filled the open basement door at the top of the stairs. "What's wrong? I thought I heard you hollering."

"Dad!" I screeched. "There's a snake down here. On the shelf. Help!"

"A what?"

I ran to the foot of the basement steps and yelled up. "A snake! I mean it. Really. Hurry up!" *Before it hides in some hole,* I added to myself. *Before it goes poof. Before it changes into a green garden hose.*

My dad hurried down the steps, then we ran toward the storage shelves.

No! My stomach lurched.

It was gone.

Then I understood. The ghost wasn't going to let an adult see it.

"Where, Clint?" Dad quickly scanned the room.

"It was behind that box!" I pointed to the carton on the shelf.

"I don't see anything, Son. Are you sure what you saw was a snake?"

"I'm sure, Dad. It was definitely a snake." My voice trembled slightly.

Dad stroked his chin with his hand. "I don't know much about snakes. Let's go back upstairs and call Mr. Rodriguez at the nature center."

"Why?" I asked. I couldn't understand how my dad could remain so calm.

"He'll be able to identify whether it's a dangerous snake. If it is, he can take it back to the nature center. If it's not, he'll know the best place to let it go."

"What if Mr. Rodriguez can't come right away? Do we just let it slither around in here?" I shivered at the thought. No way was I going to sleep in a house inhabited by a snake—or worse, a snake ghost!

"I'm not very comfortable having a snake in the basement either. If Mr. Rodriguez can't come look at it today, maybe he can tell me what to do." Dad looked up at the shelves. "Hey, there's the WD–40."

He reached for the can of oil and walked back toward the basement steps. "Come on, Clint. Let's go make that phone call. Then we can have some lunch."

I took one last look at the shelf where I'd seen the snake. Then I grabbed the string for the light switch. I was about to pull it and turn off the light when I saw movement out of the corner of my eye.

I turned my head to get a better look and gasped.

The snake had slipped from its hiding place. It had begun to wind itself around a water pipe.

The snake swung its head my direction. Its red, forked tongue began to flick. Again and again.

I knew snakes used their tongues to smell. They could sense small, warm animals that way. When they found one, they could swallow it whole.

Flick, flick, whipped the tongue.

The snake inched toward me silently.

I managed to step back. The dehumidifier droned behind me. Its sound filled my head.

Whir, plink, whir, plink.

As I watched the snake slither silently, I knew I was a goner.

I backed up farther. I jerked my head around to look behind me.

Don't stumble and fall, I told myself. *That thing knows you're trying to get it kicked out of the basement. If you turn your back on it, the snake will drop on you and take its revenge. It wants to be king down here. And you're in the way.*

That thought terrified me. I sprang into motion and raced up the steps two at a time.

I bolted through the door to the kitchen and slammed it behind me.

The aroma of spaghetti sauce and garlic bread filled the kitchen. Spaghetti is one of my favorites, but my stomach was a jumble.

Dad turned from the kitchen phone as he set it back in its cradle. "I just talked to Mr. Rodriguez. I got him on his car phone. He promised to come right over."

He can't get here soon enough, I thought.

When Mr. Rodriguez arrived, he had a burlap sack with him. He told me that he'd capture the snake and carry it back to the nature center in the sack. He guessed the snake was harmless. But he wanted to check it out thoroughly to make sure it was healthy before he set it free.

Dad took Mr. Rodriguez downstairs to show him where I had seen the snake.

I sat upstairs, restlessly pushing my lunch around on my plate with a fork. I still had no appetite. As long as that snake was in the basement, I couldn't eat.

When I heard my dad and Mr. Rodriguez climbing the steps, I jumped out of my chair.

Mr. Rodriguez entered the kitchen first, clutching the burlap bag.

"We got him, Clint." Mr. Rodriguez grinned. "It's just a harmless green snake."

Harmless? I thought. *Obviously Mr. Rodriguez didn't know about the property next to our house.*

"It's a common snake in this region," he continued. "They're not poisonous."

Dad thanked Mr. Rodriguez for coming over so quickly. Then he extended an invitation to stay and have lunch with us.

"Thank you, but I better get this little fella back to the nature center," he replied. "We'll check him to make sure he's healthy. Then we'll let him go in the grass around there."

I followed Mr. Rodriguez outside. I watched as he started up his car and drove away.

For a car carrying a ghost, it's traveling down the street just fine, I mused. It didn't suddenly speed up, veer sideways, or hit a tree. It didn't burst into a ball of flames. It didn't disappear with a poof in a cloud of smoke.

Maybe . . . just maybe . . . the snake *was* just a plain, harmless green snake.

I shrugged and went back inside to eat my lunch.

Later I called Hammer and told him about the discovery and capture of the green snake in the basement.

"Mr. Rodriguez took it back to the nature center?" Hammer asked, amazed.

"He said the snake was harmless. He planned to let it go in the grass near the nature center," I explained.

"Let it go!" Hammer nearly exploded. "Near the nature center? Where families with kids go to picnic, fish, and hike? Tell me you're kidding!"

"Hammer! Relax! It's just a harmless snake!"

I realized Hammer would really get carried away with this.

"What makes you so sure it was a harmless snake?" Hammer demanded. "What if a ghost has gotten hold of it and put it under a spell? Don't you see what that means? It's out of the swamp. It can go anywhere now. It can multiply and spread all over the world."

Hammer paused before speaking again. "This is serious. I'm on my way. We've got to think this through."

When Hammer arrived, we sat down on the front lawn.

Hammer kept looking behind us as we talked. "I've got to tell you, I'm getting the willies just sitting on this grass."

I glanced around at the innocent-looking blades of grass.

"If the snake ghosts were able to get into your basement," Hammer continued, "then they can easily invade your lawn."

Hammer spooked me too. We jumped up and ran to the concrete driveway.

"If we can't trust the lawn, what then?" Hammer asked. "Forget bushes."

"And garages," I added.

"And basements. Pipes, rafters, rain gutters—"

"And garden hoses," I said. "Hammer, we can't live like this."

"You can say that again," he agreed. "Let's get out of here for a while. Get your bike."

Hammer walked toward his bike. It was leaning against the front porch. He didn't have to step off of the concrete to get it.

I warily walked into the garage where I had parked my bike.

Looking around the garage, I began to feel nervous. There were so many places where snakes could hide. Like in back of metal shelves. Behind paint cans. Under an edge of the lawn mower. Tucked among coils of rope—or garden hose.

I looked at my bike. It leaned on the side of the garage. Dad's car stood between me and the bike. I'd have to go around it into the dim garage.

"You see something, Gleeson?" Hammer called. He had pulled his bike up outside the garage.

Go get your bike, I ordered myself. Yet with every footstep, I felt goose bumps raise on my arms.

I scanned the walls. They were smooth and white. Nothing could hide there.

I checked out the rafters . . . lots of rafters. I forced myself to enter the garage.

"Look out!" Hammer yelped from the doorway.

The hair on the back of my neck suddenly stood up.

"Behind you!" he called. "Up there! It's coming down . . . Run, Gleeson! Run!"

In a panic, I leaped in front of my dad's car and crouched there. I prayed the car would protect me. I listened intently for the snake, sure I'd hear it when it dropped, thunk, onto the car.

I began to duckwalk to my right. The floor was gritty beneath my feet. My feet skidded a bit. When my eyes were even with the headlights, I looked up. I only had to scoot around to the driver's side. Then it was a straight shot to the door.

"What is it?" I shrieked to Hammer.

"Hanging down! A whole loop of snake," he cried. "Thick as a python. Black as . . ."

I continued to inch my way around the car. "Black as what?" I asked.

No answer.

"Hammer!" Had the snake landed on Hammer and squeezed him to death?

"Clint," Hammer's voice sounded strangely calm, "get up."

71

"What? Are you okay?"

"Clint." Hammer's voice sounded sheepish. "Get up."

Slowly, I stood. But I kept my knees bent in case I had to quickly duck down again. I met Hammer's eyes. He raised his eyebrows and pointed at the ceiling.

I saw two black inner tubes stored in the rafters. One had slipped down far enough so Hammer could see it from the doorway.

I stared at the inner tubes. Then I began to giggle with relief. "Hammer, we've got to get a grip."

I ran my fingers through my hair, then continued. "Okay . . . let's think about what's happened. I found a green snake in our basement, which Mr. Rodriguez took to the nature center—"

"And if it was a ghost, the world is doomed," Hammer interrupted.

"Come on. We don't even know that ghosts live in the swamp, much less that any ghosts have come out of there. In fact, I'm not sure ghosts exist."

"So you don't think there are ghosts in the garage?" Hammer said.

"No, Hammer," I said. "And they're not in the lawn and they're not in the basement. It's all been in our imaginations."

"Those frogs were real."

Hammer had a point there. But I didn't want to think about it.

"I don't want to talk about it anymore." My voice was firm. "Let's just stay out of the swamp!"

"We leave it alone. It leaves us alone," agreed Hammer.

We walked around the house to the backyard.

Hammer sprawled in the porch swing. "I admit I feel better now."

"Yeah. We don't have to be afraid of the grass and the bushes. There's nothing there but what we created in our heads." I lay back in a lawn chair. I tried to feel confident. But deep inside, fear and uncertainty still gnawed at me.

"Feel that breeze, man." Hammer sniffed loudly. "Aaahh. Somebody's grilling outdoors."

I leaned my head back and gazed at the sky. It was as deep a blue as I'd ever seen. Huge white clouds drifted across it like proud ships. Palm leaves rattled pleasantly in the breeze.

"Take a look at that swamp grass." Hammer's voice was mellow. "Blowing every which way. Probably a bunch of ghosts stirring it up."

"Hammer, don't start," I said.

"You're right. Sorry," he answered. Hammer's eyes closed. "I sure could go for a can of soda."

"Say no more." I got up. I turned to open the door that led inside.

That was when I caught sight of a white-robed figure at the far edge of the Haunted Swamp.

The grass parted. In a twinkling, the white figure stepped through and was swallowed up. It went into a part of the swamp I hadn't explored.

"Hammer!" My voice was sharp.

"Huh?" Hammer snorted as if waking up. "What did I do?"

"Did you see . . ." I stared at the spot where I'd seen the white-robed figure vanish. "No. Of course you didn't."

"See what?" Hammer was alert now. The swing creaked as he stood up to join me.

"I'm not sure I even saw it," I mumbled, half to myself.

"Did you see something in the swamp?" Hammer asked. "If you saw it in the swamp, it doesn't matter how weird it was. In the swamp, anything goes. And we're staying out of the swamp. For good . . . So what did you think you saw?" Hammer clapped my shoulder.

"It was white and . . . billowy," I began. "The swamp grass sort of swallowed it up. It looked like . . ."

"An angel?" Hammer asked doubtfully.

"I wonder . . . ," I said after thinking a moment. "Could that be how God is going to help us fight our fears? Has he sent his angels? Think about it. When Shadrach, Meshach, and Abednego went into the fiery furnace in the Book of Daniel, they didn't go alone. We may not be facing a fiery furnace, but we're certainly in the hot seat.

"Unless . . . oh, man." I whirled around at my new thought and shoved the door open. I dashed through the breakfast room, down the hall, to the foyer. Then I pounded up the stairs and burst into Kristin's room.

She wasn't there.

I looked under the bed. Just dust bunnies and a couple of Barbie dolls.

I slid her closet door open. After rifling through the dresses, shirts, and pants, I realized she wasn't hiding there either.

I checked the bathroom, my own room, and even Mom and Dad's room, just to be sure. Kristin was not in the house.

"It was her," I said to Hammer, who had followed me into the hall. "It was Kristin. I have to go after her."

"But . . . but . . . ," Hammer stuttered. He galloped

after me as I flew down the stairs.

When I hit the first floor, I sped through the foyer, the hall, the breakfast room, and back out the back door.

I felt sweat trickle down my back. As I ran, I kept my eyes glued to the spot where Kristin had disappeared. What would I find in this new part of the swamp? And why did it seem, as I got closer, that the wind was picking up?

Gasping from exertion, I finally reached the clump of reeds where Kristin had disappeared. Up close, I was shocked to see that they were nearly as high as my head. The blades swayed before me, teasing me. The wind made an eerie whistling as it rushed past my ears.

"Kristin!" Hammer called. He had caught up with me.

If Kristin would come out, we wouldn't have to go in after her.

But she didn't answer Hammer's yell. The yellow-green spires of grass danced in front of us. They rustled and filled our ears with a hissing sound.

Was it only the grass making the sound? Or were we hearing the hissing of a thousand snake ghosts?

I shook my head to clear my thoughts. I whistled an old Amy Grant tune, "Angels Watching Over Me." I was scared, but I knew we weren't fighting this thing by ourselves.

The wind pushed me from behind. It had grown strong enough to push me a step forward. It nudged me to enter the waving grass.

"You don't have to come with me, Hammer," I said, staring at the spears of grass. "But I've got to go in there."

"Kristin!" Hammer cried again.

The sun's light dimmed. I looked up quickly. A cloud had floated in front of the sun. The wind gusted again. My T-shirt flapped at my sides. The grass had become a million green fingers beckoning me.

"If I don't go now, I might not ever," I said.

I stepped into the grass. Twigs crackled under my feet. *It's dry here, not swampy*, I thought in surprise.

The tips of the grassy weeds pricked my cheeks. The sharp blades stroked my neck. They curled on my shoulders like long fingers. *Woo, woo, woo,* the wind chugged past my ears.

"Clint!" Hammer yelped.

"I'm here!" I called back. As I twisted my shoulders, the grass surrounded me, rustling. *That is just the grass rustling, isn't it?* I thought.

"You should have seen that! The grass just ate you up!" I heard my friend call.

"I'm okay," I yelled back.

I pushed forward. One foot, then the other. There was no path here. Where had Kristin gone? I held my arms like a wedge, pushing the grass aside as I walked. My feet were lost in green tangles. When would I ever break through this clump? *Would* I break through it? "Kristin!" I yelled.

"Kristin!" Hammer's voice echoed behind me. He was trying to follow me. But the tall grass made it difficult to keep me in sight. "Gleeson! Keep talking, so I can make out where you are."

My heart pounded with fear as I called to my friend again.

The wind was furious now. It whipped the grass wildly. "I see you, man!" Hammer shouted. "That's the stuff. You're blazing a trail!"

"Kristin!" I hollered.

The tall grass abruptly came to an end. I found myself under a canopy of trees.

I continued to walk forward as I turned my head to look behind me for Hammer.

That's when I tripped.

And began tumbling, and tumbling, and tumbling.

I felt myself rolling head over heels.

I squeezed my eyes shut, afraid. My imagination took over. Was I tumbling into some sort of trap the ghosts had laid? I didn't want to see the snakes, easing their coils along beside me, flicking their tongues.

Then I stopped rolling.

For a few moments I lay there, dazed.

When I forced my eyes open, I saw that I'd landed in a mound of soft grass. It had stopped my head-over-heels fall.

I looked over my shoulder and realized I'd rolled down a giant hill.

I turned again and looked in front of me. Ten yards ahead, a tall, skinny tree reached toward the sky. The tree was dead. Its bare branches clattered against each other in the wind.

A thick strand of poison ivy climbed and wound around it. The massive vine seemed to squeeze the tree trunk like a boa constrictor squeezing its prey.

At the base of the tree I saw a large loop of green vine move. It looked like it was crawling.

A snake!

A green snake, just like the one Mr. Rodriguez had taken from the basement. Harmless? Out of the swamp, maybe. But what had Hammer said? In the swamp, anything goes.

Hammer . . . Where was he?

I whirled and jerked my head toward the top of the hill.

From above me, a voice rang down: "Gleeeeson!"

Small clods of dirt rained down from above. The dirt pelted my face. I buried my face in my arms for protection.

When I looked up again, Hammer was standing beside me.

"Hey, man," Hammer puffed.

The snake! I quickly faced the tree.

The snake was gone.

"Which way would Kristin go?" Hammer asked.

"Who knows?" I shook my head. My thoughts were jumbled. I gazed at the greenery surrounding us. Except for the dead tree, the land was wild with leaves and vines.

Thinking out loud, I murmured, "She'd go where the story is."

"Oh, man, you are giving me the creeps," Hammer said. "Make sense, will you?"

"She must be at the cabin." The wind snatched my words away. "That's got to be to our right."

We began to trudge through the plants and bushes. Even this deep in the swamp, the wind continued to whip against us. It blew so hard and steadily that we had to fight to stand.

"We weren't expecting a hurricane, were we?" Hammer yelled.

"The sky was clear and sunny earlier this afternoon," I answered.

"Well, we're in the swamp now. Anything can happen here," Hammer said. "Is it my imagination, or is it getting darker?"

"It looks like it's getting darker. We've got to hurry and find Kristin. If a storm's blowing in, we could get trapped in here."

We had only managed to struggle a few yards past the dead tree. I stepped carefully, sure that snake was close by.

"Kristin!" I yelled. While we walked west, the wind blew my words south. When I called my sister, it was like yelling in two directions at once.

Oooooooooh, the wind moaned through the trees.

"I didn't know wind could blow so hard," Hammer said.

Because it's not just wind, I thought. *It's ghosts' breath.* Then I remembered there's a mightier wind than this. Spirit means "wind." When the Holy Spirit blows, the snake ghosts better watch out!

I spotted something gauzy and white fluttering in the breeze up ahead. As we got closer I stopped suddenly in my tracks, horrified by what I saw on the ground.

The wind tugged and pulled at glossy blond hair on the ground, tossing it like corn silk.

"Oh, man," Hammer moaned.

I opened my mouth. But not even a croak came out.

I stumbled forward.

In front of us Kristin lay motionless on the ground.

17

"Kristin!" The name burst from my lips. The grass hissed like a nest of vipers as I crouched at her side.

Her ice blue eyes stared up at me.

I felt tears well up in my eyes. What had the ghosts done to my baby sister?

Kristin sat up.

I shuddered and jumped back. Hammer screamed.

Something about Kristin's expression looked unnatural. Suddenly I understood. The ghosts had turned my sister into one of their zombies.

I scrambled to my feet. My legs tingled. My bones felt like sponges.

Kristin stood and took a step forward. Hammer and I took a step backward.

Kristin blinked her eyes. The wind whipped her hair around her face. She looked normal now. And her face looked very angry.

I scrunched mine up to match her expression.

"Just what were you trying to pull? I thought you were hurt!"

Kristin began to cry. The wind snatched at her dress. "You spoiled it again."

"What? What did I spoil?" My throat felt raw. "Come on, Kristin." I reached for her. "Don't cry. Let's go home. Maybe Mom's there."

"Nuh-uh." Kristin scrubbed at her face with both fists. She straightened her white dress and shook her blond hair. Then she turned and ran—deeper into the swamp.

Rustling sounds filled the air. We charged after her. But in only seconds, we had lost sight of her. Again we had no idea which way Kristin had gone.

Hammer stopped running.

I stopped too.

The wind snatched leaves from the bushes, vines, and plants around us, flinging them through the air. The leaves swirled and slapped at our faces.

"The ghosts are ripping this place apart," Hammer croaked.

"Yeah." The word squeaked out of my throat. "I guess they're done with it."

"And with everything in it."

I shuddered.

"And you know what that means." Hammer's whisper was harsh. "De-struc-tion!"

Just then lightning flashed. Seconds later thunder rumbled overhead.

"The storm's here!" Hammer yelled. "Which way do we go?"

"The cabin!" I said. I pointed ahead.

Side by side, we entered the darkest part of the swamp. Here the tall treetops had all grown together. The branches swayed wildly in the violent wind.

How, I wondered, will we ever find our way? We had never tried to find the cabin from this direction. And now it was getting dark.

And what if we found our way, only to discover that Kristin wasn't there? That she had lost her way?

Lightning flashed again, glowing through the ceiling of green leaves. In that instant, I thought I saw shadows closing in on us.

The ghosts have surrounded us!

A clap of thunder made Hammer scream.

I suddenly noticed something flying through the air. It slammed into my right shoulder and sent me stumbling into the swishing grass beyond.

"Hey, Clint." Lying in the grass, I heard Hammer speak. At least, I thought it was Hammer.

Something had knocked me over. Then the weight of a body had landed on me.

"Ooof. Hammer! Help!" I yelled to my friend.

"Gleeson?"

"Hammer! Over here!" I said. "Did it get you too?"

"No. But that tree limb really smacked you good. This wind is pretty wild."

Hammer helped me to my feet. We tried to orient ourselves toward the cabin again. As we worked our way around the trees, we brushed damp nets of low-hanging leaves out of our faces.

A low, deep rumbling sounded overhead. It seemed to shake the earth.

"If this is a storm, then where's the rain?" Hammer grunted.

I shook my head. There were no sensible answers. Maybe this wasn't a storm. So who could say the rumbling was thunder? The ghosts could be blowing up the ground beneath our feet.

We reached a small clearing. We could see the clouds above us.

The sky had become a ceiling of gray-black thunderheads. Then a whole network of lightning split the sky into a jigsaw puzzle. Thunder shook our ears, our hearts, the whole earth. And then the rain poured down.

We instinctively crouched in the clearing so we wouldn't attract the lightning. Water poured down on us, soaking our clothes, our shoes. Our dripping hair was plastered against our heads. Lightning flashed around us like a fireworks show. Each deafening peal of thunder made my stomach leap. We did not dare go into the trees now.

I could only guess at what might be happening to Kristin.

Neither of us had on a watch. We had no idea how long the rain lasted. But after a while, the drops no longer ping-ping-pinged against us.

I looked at Hammer. He was as wet as if he'd gone swimming in the Gulf with his clothes on. Hammer's black hair looked like it had been painted on.

I was sure I looked as bad. I gazed down at my T-shirt and saw how it stuck to my body.

We craned our necks toward the patch of sky above the clearing. The clouds were starting to break up.

The air smelled earthy. Rain trickled from leaves all around. It sounded like a million dripping faucets.

I pointed forward, and we waded into the thick trees again. At once we were showered by water drops from the leaves.

My courage rose when I saw that the trees were starting to look familiar. We must have crossed into the swamp near the cabin. The jail tree couldn't be far ahead. Then we'd only have a little way to go to reach the cabin.

All of a sudden Hammer scuffed to a stop. He grabbed my arm and pointed at something ahead of us.

Something white, thin, and limp had snagged on a low branch just ahead. It looked soaked by the rain.

I knew instantly what it was.

That fine, white fabric tangled in the tree was a piece of Kristin's dress.

19

"She got away." Hammer squeaked like a mouse.

I knew his words were meant for comfort. Kristin had freed herself from the tree—a tree that could have been struck by lightning.

Or maybe she didn't free herself. Maybe she had been taken away. I pushed that thought away. I ran to the tree and grabbed hold of the cloth.

It was the skirt of Kristin's dress. I thought about how long and hard she must have struggled to tear it off.

I tugged at the cloth.

The branch tugged back.

I got a better hold on the cloth and tried to work it loose. But the branch seemed to have countless twigs sprouting from its ends. Every one of them had burrowed its way into the filmy cloth.

"Hey," Hammer said, "leave it there. Let's go look for Kristin."

We got our bearings then ran as fast as we could through the snares of vines and the juts of uneven ground that tried to trip us. All the trees shook water from their leaves on us as we passed. Low hanging clumps of leaves smacked our faces like wet mops.

The jail tree loomed ahead.

Scrambling toward it, I scanned between its vines for a sign of my sister.

We stopped short of the jail tree. For some reason it appeared even more menacing today.

Its countless arms waved. Its countless knotholes, looking like wooden eye sockets, stared. It dared us to search it, to take our chances in its prison of vines.

I turned my face away.

"I've got to go in and look for Kristin. What if she didn't make it to the cabin before the rain started? She might have gone in there to stay dry," I said.

"Don't, Clint. I think it would be a mistake." Hammer's face was grim.

"No, you don't. You'd do the same if your sister had disappeared. I know you would."

Our eyes locked. Hammer nodded.

Then I slipped beneath the jail tree.

The door to the tunnel that we'd found before stood open. I had to explore it, just in case Kristin had fled there. Once inside the tunnel, it seemed I had entered a new dimension of time and space. Complete darkness engulfed me, and I took a few moments to let my eyes adjust.

But as soon as I could see, I wished I couldn't. I wasn't alone.

Two eyes stared directly into mine.

"Kristin?" I whispered.

My breath became short and rapid. The beady eyes remained fixed on me and didn't answer. I didn't dare move.

Eventually I realized I couldn't hold my cramped position any longer. The rain had penetrated the jail tree. The walls of the tunnel were damp and slippery. I knew as soon as I tried to move I'd probably skid down the tunnel—and who knew what else waited for me down there? Would I ever see my family again? Would anyone ever find Kristin?

I had to make my move suddenly, to take those horrible beady eyes by surprise. With a quick prayer in my heart, I inhaled sharply and thrashed into the darkness, hoping to protect myself against the evil in the tunnel.

I connected with soft, vulnerable body parts. In fact, the being was nothing but softness. I found myself grappling with a teddy bear.

What was a teddy bear doing in a moss-covered

tunnel in the middle of a vine-covered tree in the heart of an overgrown swamp?

I peered farther into the darkness. And I saw other beady eyes, other bears.

"Kristin?" I called again softly. "Kristin, are you here?"

I pushed aside the bears and felt my way down the tunnel. It branched off, and I decided to follow the left option.

I wished I had a ball of string, remembering my concern for Tom Sawyer during his spelunking adventures. I could very easily become lost in the darkness and never find my way out.

"Kristin?"

A few feet later, I came to a wooden door and tried to pull it open. It was locked. I had no choice but to back up and try the right hand passage.

That tunnel led to another door. I could see that it was open just a crack. Cool, refreshing air drifted through it. I was about to check it out when I heard hissing sounds and laughter on the other side. The voices were getting closer.

No time to lose, I thought. Quickly I scrambled back toward the tunnel entrance and ducked behind the bears clustered there.

My timing had been dangerously close. A ghostly figure drifted past me just as I slipped out of sight. I didn't dare go deep into the tunnel to continue my search. I longed for the world of daylight and green trees.

When Hammer saw me emerge from the jail tree, his face was pale with fright.

"Man, am I ever glad to see you!" he said. Overjoyed, he threw his arms around my neck. "Who came out of the tunnel before you? I was sure he'd had lunch down there and that you'd been the main course. I was afraid he'd turn me into dessert. What did you find in there?"

"This doesn't make sense, Hammer. The tunnel was packed with teddy bears! And at the end of the tunnel, I heard hissing and other sounds, so I ran out of there. But I didn't find Kristin." I felt a lump rising in my throat.

"Teddy bears? . . . Hissing? . . . What's going on here?" Hammer asked. Then he saw the concern on my face and added, "Don't give up yet. There's still the cabin. I'm sure we'll find Kristin."

Hammer mopped his face with the edge of his wet T-shirt. But it was like trying to dry off after a swim with a towel that had fallen into the pool. "We are just about there. Right? To the cabin?"

"Nothing between us and it except this tree and a hill," I answered. "A small hill."

"The way things are going, it might as well be a mountain. Is it just me, or does it feel as if we've been in here for about two weeks?"

"It's not just you," I said slowly.

We'd gone through a kind of night and day, with the storm. I began to wonder just how late it was.

Could it be that the swamp was not only slowly encroaching, eating our yard but that it also was swallowing time? How much of our lives would be eaten up here before we finally got free?

Hammer shook himself and said, "Come on. Let's find your sister and get out of here. If Kristin's not at the cabin, maybe we should go for help."

I nodded in agreement, and we raced past the jail tree. We got all the way to the top of the hill without anything unusual happening. We looked down at the cabin.

Its charred wood was almost black after being drenched by the rain. The thick underbrush that hulked close to it made lumpy shadows.

Hammer hissed, "That's got to be the ghosts' headquarters."

"A tunnel under the floor," I remembered out loud.

"Zillions of frogs," Hammer reminded me.

The frogs had been real. We'd both seen the frogs.

I started down the hill. Hammer kept pace.

"We'll look in all the windows," I suggested. "Let's start on this side. Next the back window, straight across from the door. Then the other side—if we need to."

I took a deep breath. The last part of my plan scared me. "If we can't see anything through the windows, we'll have to try the door."

Hammer didn't reply. He stood staring wide-eyed, focused somewhere behind me.

I saw that Hammer's lips were pressed together tightly. His face, under his black hair, looked bleached. He looked as if he had seen . . . a ghost!

21

I spun around to face the cabin.

I saw a soaked little girl racing toward me. Her blond hair hung limp and stringy. A ragged, filmy white top covered her T-shirt. Pink flowered shorts clung damply to her wet knees. She regarded me with wide-eyed silence.

"Kristin!" Relief bubbled through me. "Are you okay?"

She didn't answer.

"Kristin? You are okay, right? Where were you when it was raining so hard? Did you get hurt?"

Kristin opened her mouth. Then she burst into tears. "I was so scared. The thunder hurt my ears," she wailed. "And I tried to run but a big tree grabbed me. I pulled and pulled, but it wouldn't let go. It tore my dress."

I held my little sister, patting her back until her sobbing subsided.

She sniffled and looked up at me. "It's not even the right day," she said. "Did you know that?"

"What are you talking about?" I asked.

But I guessed what Kristin was talking about. Time in the swamp seemed much different from time in the world outside it. The longer we were trapped here, the bigger and wilder the time difference became. Kristin believed we were now on a whole different day.

"I know how to get the right day back," I told her. "All we have to do is go home."

Kristin frowned as she studied my face. "How is going home going to help it be the right day?" she asked.

"Well," I began, "I think the day that's out there must be the right day. Because the enchanted forest is the only place where the day is different. In every other place, the time is the same. Understand?"

Kristin thought hard about this for a moment, then understanding lit her face. "Ooooohhh. 'Course. The 'chanted forest has different days. But that's okay. I meant it's the wrong day for me to be Goldilocks. The wrong day again. See, first it rained and I got all wet . . ."

"Goldilocks doesn't get wet in the story?" I prompted. I tried to nudge Kristin toward the little hill while we talked. She didn't budge.

"A tree doesn't rip her dress in the story either. I ran to the Three Bears' house to hide from the thunder." Kristin was speaking rapidly. "But when I got here, the Three Bears were home." Kristin flapped her hand toward the cabin. "And Goldilocks doesn't go in when they're home. Because that's not in the story."

"What?" I blinked. I reached out and gripped Kristin by the arm.

Hammer made a gurgling sound.

"Clinty, what are you doing? You're squeezing my arm," Kristin complained.

"What was that about the Three Bears?" I loosened my grip.

"The Three Bears are home," Kristin said again. "They must be done with the porridge. 'Cause now it's sitting time. They're sitting in their chairs. One, two, three in a row. Go look if you don't believe me."

I met Hammer's eyes.

"Go look, Clinty," Kristin repeated.

Hammer and I ran to the cabin. It couldn't be. I was sure we wouldn't see three bears sitting on chairs. It wasn't possible.

Yet thousands of frogs appearing overnight didn't seem possible either. But we had seen them.

The windows were streaked with rivers of mud from the storm. Together, we propped our foreheads on the glass. We cupped our hands around our eyes. We peered inside.

And screamed.

In the middle of the cabin, three bears sat on a row of chairs.

"This can't be," whimpered Hammer.

I felt weak. I thought I should sit down. But I couldn't. I knew that if I took my eyes off them, the bears might disappear. Or they could turn into frogs. I had to keep standing. I had to keep looking.

Once again it was too dark in the cabin to see the floor clearly. I couldn't see if there was a hole in the floor leading to a tunnel.

"They look stuffed," Hammer commented.

"Like the ones in the tunnel," I added.

"And they're all the same size. No Papa, Mama, and Baby bear."

The bears were just giant toys. Their fur seemed to be brown or black. Around the edges they looked ratty, like they were old, well-used toys.

"Even if they aren't real bears, what are they doing in there? I mean, how did they get there?" I asked.

"Just what I was wondering," Hammer whispered.

"And where are the frogs?" I felt myself grow more nervous as we continued to stand there. "Hammer, this cabin was full of frogs yesterday."

"Maybe they went through the hole in the floor. Maybe they're in the tunnel." Hammer looked at the ground beneath his feet. "The frogs could be under there now." He looked back through the window.

"But what do snake ghosts need with hundreds of frogs in the first place?" I asked. "And why would they set up toy bears in an abandoned cabin?"

Hammer didn't have an answer.

"Let's look around. Maybe there's another tunnel entrance nearby," he finally said.

While I kept Kristin in sight, we spent some time searching the bushes near the cabin for a tunnel opening. Perhaps there was some overgrowth blocking an entrance, maybe a tall bush that seemed out of place. But it was just too hard to tell. The rain had turned everything wet and soggy.

"This isn't getting us anywhere," I finally said. "I think we should go inside."

"Inside the cabin?" Hammer asked, incredulous.

I knew what Hammer was thinking. I was also wondering how dangerous it might be to go into the cabin. If there really was a ghosts' tunnel underneath, we might be stepping directly into harm's way.

"Look, what choice do we have? There's something really strange going on here. You and I both know that it isn't going to stop unless we come up with the courage to figure out what it is. For some reason, we've seen something nobody else has.

"We can't go to the police. What could we tell them? That there are teddy bears and a secret tunnel next door? We just have to handle this on our own."

My words hung in the air between us. Having said them, I now had to act.

"Okay, I'm going in." But my feet felt like lead as I walked toward the door. It's one thing to say you have courage and quite another to actually have it. I turned back to Hammer. "At the first sign of trouble, you grab Kristin and beat it!"

Hammer nodded solemnly and clutched my little sister's hand.

It seemed to take an eternity to get to the door of the cabin. My fingers worked and my palms sweated as I contemplated the knob. There was no putting it off.

I tried the knob, not knowing whether I wanted it to be locked or not.

It turned easily.

The door swung back on its hinges.

I half expected screeches and screams to come from within. But I didn't hear a sound. My trespassing had gone unnoticed. All that greeted me were three dopey-looking stuffed bears perched on chairs.

Hammer ventured to peek around the doorjamb. "Clint?"

"Come on in. The coast is clear," I responded.

Hammer cautiously entered the cabin with Kristin in tow.

"Let's check this place out. If you find anything, don't touch it. Let's just make note of anything unusual."

"Right," Hammer agreed.

Slowly we began to scour the one-room cabin. We found no signs of a tunnel beneath the table. There were no loose boards. No knotholes triggered springs to open hidden passageways. The windows were shut tight and locked. I wondered why the door had been unlocked.

"This is crazy," Hammer said. "Bears coming and going and coming again. Frogs appearing and disappearing. You and I both know there were frogs in here. And now there's no sign of them."

I barely heard my friend. The bears had grabbed my full attention. Something very strange was happening to them.

A bulge began to form in one arm of the bear on the left. Right below its shoulder.

"Can a toy move like that?" Hammer whined when he realized what I was staring at.

I didn't know what to say.

The bulge rippled.

"I've never seen a bear with muscles like that," Hammer said. His voice rose high and stayed there.

"Me either," I agreed. I could hear the panic rising in my voice too.

"What about ghost bears?" he asked.

"Who knows? Are there any rules for ghost bears?" I asked.

"Well?"

The reedy voice behind me made me jump.

"Well?" Kristin's voice shrilled again. "Now do you believe me about the Three Bears?"

"Yeah," Hammer squeaked.

"Take my hand, Kristin," I commanded, without taking my eyes off the squirming bear.

"But I want to see the Three Bears," my sister said, pouting. She wasn't tall enough to see over my shoulder, and I didn't want her to know the bears were flexing their muscles. If she thought the bears were alive, she might fall back into the story.

"Not right now, Kristin. Remember, they're at home. They're not supposed to see Goldilocks," I urged. I maneuvered her toward the door and motioned for Hammer to follow us. But Hammer was mesmerized by the bears.

"The ghosts must have made these bears pump iron," Hammer chattered nervously. "Oh, man, look at that!"

The stomach of the bear on the right had begun to bulge.

I knew we had to get out of there. But my knees had suddenly turned to jelly.

At the same time, a huge bump began to grow on the top of the middle bear's head.

"Nobody," Hammer panted, "but nobody, has a muscle like that on his skull."

"Look!" I said in alarm. I pointed to the bear with the bulging arm. Another arm was slowly growing out of the bulge. It was just a tiny arm, though. Skinny. But long. And hairless. Dark, shadowy, rubbery, it kept coming . . .

"Snake!" cried Hammer.

At that moment, the second bear's belly exploded.

Snakes poured onto the floor. I couldn't tell how many there were. I couldn't even tell the head of one from the tail of another. The snakes flopped and wriggled over one another as they burst out of the mangy bear.

We wasted no more time in the cabin. I snatched Kristin up and ran for dear life. Hammer followed close behind.

We ran for what seemed like hours before we finally came to a clearing and fell to our hands and knees, breathless.

"We . . . can't stop," Hammer wheezed. "The tunnel . . . We didn't find the entrance . . . but . . . those snakes know where it is . . . That means they could get out of the cabin, underground. That means they could pop up . . . anywhere. They could pop up just anywhere . . . Let's beat it."

I turned to Kristin. I was about to grab her arm and run when an eerie cackle pierced the air.

Kristin screamed and grabbed my leg.

"Run!" Hammer yelped. "Whatever that was, it's close!"

Hammer took off running. I took Kristin's hand and began to run so fast that I practically dragged her behind me.

The loud, ghostly cackle sounded again.

I risked a quick glance over my shoulder.

And I caught a glimpse of something stepping out from behind one of the trees.

I didn't stop to get a better look. It seemed smarter to keep running, pulling Kristin along behind me.

Hammer reached the edge of our yard first.

Kristin and I scrambled out of the deep weeds just as Hammer was climbing onto his bike.

Gasping for breath, Hammer stammered, "I've . . . got to . . . get . . . away . . . from here." He tried to inhale deeply. "Call me . . . later."

Panting heavily, I watched as my friend pedaled furiously away.

Kristin started to cry. *She's tired and confused,* I thought, trying not to get upset with her for fussing.

I took Kristin into the house and calmed her down. Then I went to my bedroom and threw myself on the bed, staring at the ceiling. I discovered I was still trembling.

I tried to focus on what I'd seen after the ghostly cackle. I'd only caught a brief glimpse, but I was certain I had not seen a snake. I was pretty sure I'd seen a man.

This was nuts. Nothing made sense. Frogs appeared overnight and then disappeared just as quickly. Teddy bears loaded with snakes. A shrill cackle and a mysterious man. What was going on?

My mind was racing with questions, but I couldn't come up with any answers.

"I need a soda," I said out loud, startling myself with my voice. *Get a grip,* I added silently as I dragged myself off the bed.

On my way to the kitchen, I had to walk through the family room. Mom and Dad were watching the evening news.

Kristin was curled up in Dad's lap. She appeared to be sleeping.

As I passed through the room, a newscaster said something that grabbed my attention. I forgot about my soda for a moment and sat down in front of the TV.

I rarely watched the news, but this particular report was fascinating. I listened intently.

When the report was over, I went to the kitchen for my drink. Then I sat down and began thinking carefully about what had happened in the swamp.

I prayed for guidance as a plan began to form.

After supper, I called Hammer and told him about my plan. I needed my friend to take another trip into the swamp with me.

"I'm not sure, Gleeson," Hammer said. "It could be dangerous."

"Not if we stick to my plan. Meet me here tomorrow at ten o'clock," I urged.

Hammer hesitated at first. Finally he said, "Okay. If you're sure this will work."

"I'm sure," I answered. "I'm sure."

Hammer was right on time the next morning. I went over my plan a second time to make sure we both understood.

"Remember, we have to stay on the path to the cabin," I said again.

"Right," Hammer agreed.

We stepped into the tall grass at the edge of the swamp. Then we made our way to the path that led to the cabin.

"I sure hope we don't run into any cackling ghosts today," Hammer said loudly.

"Or any snakes," I replied, just as loud.

We passed the jail tree and began to climb the little hill.

"Listen," I whispered. I stopped and concentrated on the sounds around us.

"What is it?" Hammer had stopped beside me.

"I thought I heard a voice."

We both strained to hear.

Suddenly a loud cackle of laughter filled the still air. We screamed simultaneously.

When we looked up, we saw a tall, gangly form at the top of the hill.

"So you've come back to join usssss," it hissed.

I realized I was sweating. For a second I began to doubt my plan.

"I hope you can run fassst today," the voice said as bright eyes glared at us. "Because if you don't, you will ssstay here with usssss forever." It threw back its head and released another ghostly cackle.

But I knew this was no ghost.

"Freeze!" another voice shouted.

The ghostly form tried to run, but someone grabbed it from behind and wrestled it to the ground.

"Good work, boys." A police officer stepped into view. Another officer, the one who had wrestled the "ghost" to the ground, now had him in handcuffs.

"Clint!" Dad came out from behind a clump of bushes where he had been anxiously watching my plan unfold. He rushed over to hug me.

"We have the second smuggler in cuffs down by the cabin," an officer said. "If it hadn't been for you kids, these guys might never have been caught."

"That's right," another officer said. "They would have hustled out of here and moved their little game somewhere else."

"I wouldn't have made the connection if I hadn't seen that report about smugglers on the news last night," I offered. "When the report listed the kinds of animals being smuggled—you know, frogs from South America, exotic reptiles—I realized it might be happening right here in our swamp."

I wiped beads of sweat from my forehead.

"When the report said the smugglers often hid the animals by sewing them into suitcase linings, or even stuffed animals, all the confusing things we'd seen suddenly made sense."

"Apparently somebody didn't sew those bears we saw well enough," Hammer added. "And blammo! Snake explosion."

"The cabin was their pickup point," an officer confirmed. "They played on the local fears that there were ghosts haunting the swamp.

"And it almost worked. If they had cleared out early this morning, they probably would have gotten away."

Dad put one arm around my shoulder and the other around Hammer's. "Come on, guys. I think you heroes deserve a special lunch."

I looked at Hammer and gave him a high five. Then we all walked down the path toward home.

The crowd applauded and cameras flashed as the mayor shook my hand. The mayor offered his hand to Hammer as well. There had already been a couple of articles in the newspaper about our adventures in the swamp. Now there would be another covering our award ceremony.

"These are indeed fine examples of today's youth," the mayor intoned. "We hear a lot these days about the irresponsibility of our children and their declining moral values, but here we have two young men who, out of concern for their community, faced their fears and overcame them."

I had tried to explain that I wasn't brave at all. I had prayed and relied on the Lord to protect me. I hoped my message got through, especially to kids my age. I knew that without the Lord by my side, I'd have never been able to carry out the plan and crack the smuggling operation.

Hammer felt the same way. He was attending youth group more often these days, and it seemed that every time I turned around, Hammer was reading his Bible.

My parents still plan to buy the property next door, of course. They want to fix up the cabin to rent out as a one-room bed-and-breakfast. It could be really cute. As part of the renovation, the tunnels will be filled in and the grounds landscaped and made safe. Needless to say, the name Haunted Swamp is here to stay, and I expect I'll have to tell our bed-and-breakfast guests about my adventures.

Sometimes Hammer and I still retreat to the jail tree. It has turned out to be a great hideaway.

"Things sure have changed since we caught the smugglers, haven't they, Hammer?" I asked one day while we lounged near the jail tree tunnel.

"I'll say," he answered. "You know, I love the jail tree and all that . . ."

"Um-huh?" I prompted absently.

"And the cabin's a great place to hang out when there's nobody around . . ."

"Right . . . so why do I hear a 'but' coming?" I asked.

"There's just one thing I don't think I'll ever get used to," he stated.

"What's that, Hammer?"

"Teddy bears," he said with a grin. "If I ever see another one as long as I live, it will be too soon."

**Read and collect all of
Fred E. Katz's**

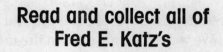

SpineChillers™
Mysteries

*Turn the page
for a spine-chilling preview . . .*

Tuck Me In, Mummy

Book #9
by Fred E. Katz

We looked at each other. I could see the fear on my friends' faces. We were the only ones in the museum. My dad was working downstairs, and none of us could have made the sounds. *Lord,* I prayed, *What do I do now? We're scared. I'm sure that Daniel was frightened when he was in the lions' den, but you protected him. Protect us too.*

We needed to do something. "I'm going to go find out what's making noise out there," I whispered as softly as I could. I didn't want my voice to give away my plan. Before I could leave the group, Benjamin touched my arm. He was unwinding the bandages as fast as he could.

"Sis, I don't think you should go out there alone," he said.

"Does that mean you want to come with me?"

"No, it doesn't mean that. I'm not sure any of us should go out there. Besides, it could just be a mouse," he told me.

"An awfully big mouse," Becca said doubtfully. Then she stiffened her body to give herself strength. "Jessica is right. Someone has to go out there. If she's going, then so am I." Becca slipped out of her sleeping bag. Together we stepped toward the doorway. We heard two more sets of steps behind us. The boys were coming too.

I stuck my head out of the entrance. I couldn't see anything moving, and the sound had stopped. "Whatever it was, it seems to be gone. Maybe we had better go out there and take a better look."

Benjamin softly responded, "When we walk out, Becca can go straight ahead and check the room over there. Adam, turn to your left and slip along the wall over there. Jessica, go to the right. I'll go around behind the pyramid. If Tut is out there, one of us will see him. When you do—scream. I don't think any of us want to tangle with Tut by ourselves."

Each of us nodded our heads in agreement. Becca and Adam crept out first. The museum had grown darker. The dim lighting made everything harder to see. Most forms were misty silhouettes. I couldn't tell what they were until I was nearly on top of them. Fortunately, none of them turned out to be Tut. That was a relief.

I circled around the room being as quiet as possible. I still heard nothing, and I hoped that nothing heard me. My steps were soft, but on the hard floor it was nearly impossible to creep along without making some noise. I turned the corner and crossed in front of a mummy. Was it real or another model? I couldn't tell in the dark. I stared at it and held my breath. If the linen-wrapped body was Tut's, then I might be joining him in the great beyond. But there was no movement.

Clink! It sounded like a small metal object had fallen to the floor. I looked away from the mummy to see where the noise had come from. Then I looked back quickly. I was sure the mummy had shifted its weight to the other foot. But I was also sure that this mummy could not walk the earth. It must have been my imagination.

Imagination or not, I was so scared that goose bumps popped up all over my body. The hair on the back of my neck prickled. I wasn't sure that I liked this type of mystery. It was a little too real.

I turned the corner and headed toward where I heard the metal drop. After a few steps I could feel the presence of someone else in the room. My heart started pounding in my throat. *Father in heaven, please help me! Take this fear out of me, and save me from anything evil here.* I was spinning around to see who was there when a hand grabbed my arm. I opened my mouth to scream, and Becca stepped in front of me.

She whispered in a frightened voice, "Sorry to scare you, but when you walked in, I thought you were a mummy. To be honest, I'm scared, really scared."

Softly I told her, "So am I. It looks like there's nothing here. We should head back to the pyramid and see what the boys discovered."

We retraced my steps to the pyramid. When we came around the corner, something looked different. For a moment, I couldn't put my finger on it. Like a bolt of lightning, the realization went off in my brain. The mummy I saw before was gone!

I pulled Becca to a dead stop. "I don't want to scare you any more than you are, but when I was coming into your room to see what fell, I walked by a mummy. It was standing right on that platform. He isn't there anymore."

"Are you sure?"

"Yeah, I'm sure. As sure as I know you dropped something metal in your room," I responded, trying to make my point without raising my voice.

"Then he wasn't there, because I was also heading toward that noise. I thought you dropped something," she exclaimed, raising our fear several notches. I could feel cold sweat on my forehead as my breath came in quick gasps.

We turned and scanned the room, but in the darkness just about everything looked like a monster. In another second we bolted for the pyramid entrance and went diving inside to where our sleeping bags were.

"Grab your flashlight, Becca. We need to get some light in the dark corners and shadows," I ordered.

Both of us dug through our bags, but neither of us found flashlights.

Becca gave me a puzzled look and said, "I know that I left mine in here. I saw it just before we left."

"Then Tut's been in here. He's probably heading to the caskets below. We've got to go find the boys," I told her. We leaped to our feet. I was almost out the entrance when I crashed into a figure coming in.

I would have screamed except that Benjamin said something before I could. "Jessica, what's going on? I heard you running to the pyramid. Did you see something?"

"It's what we didn't see," I told him. "First I saw a mummy, and then it was gone. A second ago we were looking for our flashlights, and we can't find them anywhere. We think Tut has been here and taken them. He could be in the burial chamber right now."

"Do you think that we should go down there and find out?" Becca fearfully inquired.

"I guess so," my brother told her. Adam screamed for help. Tut had him! We froze with fright.